Falling for a Cowboy's Legacy

Vargas Ranch Book 8

Karen Baney

desert life
media

Falling for a Cowboy's Legacy: Vargas Ranch Book 8
By Karen Baney

Unless otherwise indicated, all Scripture quotations are from the Christian Standard Bible®, Copyright © 2017 by Holman Bible Publishers. Used by permission. Christian Standard Bible® and CSB® are federally registered trademarks of Holman Bible Publishers.

Scripture quotations marked ESV have been taken from The ESV® Bible (The Holy Bible, English Standard Version®), copyright © 2001 by Crossway, a publishing ministry of Good News Publishers. Used by permission. All rights reserved.

Publisher:
Desert Life Media, LLC
Gilbert, AZ 85295

www.karenbaney.com

Printed in the United States of America

ISBN 978-1-960217-53-0

With regard to the works of man,
by the word of your lips
I have avoided the ways of the violent.
My steps have held fast to your paths;
my feet have not slipped.

— Psalms 17:4-5 ESV

1

SUNDAY SUPPER WAS a tradition, and Devon Vargas wouldn't miss it for anything. Not just because Mami's cooking was legendary, but because it was the one time each week the family gathered, shared stories, and connected over their roots.

The family ranch house buzzed with laughter and conversation, plates stacked high with enchiladas, tamales, and green chile pork—one of Papi's personal favorites. Devon was just finishing off his second helping when Papi cleared his throat, pulling everyone's attention toward him.

"It's going to be a busy fall," he said, leaning back in his chair. "We should plan carefully with the resort's off-season. And Mami and I want everything ready for Vargas Ranch's eightieth anniversary."

Devon sat up a little straighter. Eighty years. Eight decades since Dalton Sr. and Maria first put down roots in Arizona.

"That's huge," Dalton said from across the table. "We should do something big for it."

Several voices chimed in with ideas—an anniversary gala, a special rodeo event, a community service project to give back—but Devon's mind was already spinning in a different direction.

The history.

"You know, we should document it." His voice cut

through the chatter, and he turned toward Papi, who had been quiet, sipping coffee. "We talk about our family history, but how much of it do we actually have written down?"

Devon's wife Raina handed their antsy four-year-old to him. He whispered a request to settle down before setting Cliff's feet back on the ground.

Papi raised an eyebrow. "Padre told plenty of stories."

"Yeah, but stories fade. Details get lost." Devon leaned forward. "Think about it, Papi. We have generations' worth of history tied to Vargas Ranch. Dalton Sr. starting it with Maria. Padre's contributions. Everything you did to expand it. And now, all of us are carrying pieces of that legacy forward in different ways."

A murmur of agreement spread around the table.

"*Muy bueno!*" Mami said, nodding. "A lot of history worth preserving, no?"

"I'd read it," Drake added, earning giggles from his wife, Candi.

Papi scratched his beard. "I might have some old records and letters. When we cleared out Padre's room, we boxed up a lot of things. Could be useful."

That was all Devon needed to hear. His pulse kicked up at the thought of digging through decades of history, uncovering stories that even Papi might not fully remember.

As the rest of the family finished their plates and began filtering out, Devon stayed behind. He caught Raina's hand, gave her a quick kiss, then murmured, "I'll catch up with you later."

She smiled knowingly. "I know that look—you're already lost in research mode. Just don't stay up all night."

Devon laughed and turned back to Papi, who was stacking plates. "So, what do you say? Want to dig through the Vargas family history with me?"

Papi eyed him for a long moment, then nodded. "Let's see what we find."

TRES STOOD IN the storage room, arms crossed, eyeing the stacks of old boxes like a man staring down a herd of cattle he wasn't sure he had the patience to wrangle.

"Not even sure what all is in here," he muttered, nudging a dust-covered lid with the toe of his boot. "Been sitting untouched for years."

Devon, already rolling up his sleeves, grinned. "That just makes it more exciting."

Tres huffed but grabbed a crate, dragging it toward the center of the room. The storage shed was warm and stale, the Arizona sun pressing against the corrugated metal walls. The air smelled faintly of wood, dust, and time—a forgotten history waiting to be disturbed.

"You get excited too easy," Tres muttered, shaking his head.

Devon ignored him, cutting the tape on the first box with his pocketknife. He carefully lifted the flaps, revealing yellowed envelopes, ranch logs, and old photographs stacked haphazardly inside.

Tres squatted next to him, picking up a sepia-toned photo of Padre as a young man, standing beside Maria in front of the ranch house. She looked strong, proud—a woman who had lived through enough to know faith was the only certainty in life.

Devon pulled out an envelope, eyes widening. "These look like letters."

Tres leaned in. Dalton Sr.'s handwriting.

Devon scanned the date. "1941. This was during World War II."

Tres frowned, shifting his weight. He had always thought of his grandparents' life starting in Arizona in 1952—the year they established Vargas Ranch. Padre had shared plenty of stories about their faith, their love, their commitment to building something lasting. But he had never mentioned their early years.

Devon carefully pulled out the first letter, his fingers tracing the faded ink. "I don't think anyone's read these in decades."

Tres exhaled slowly, gripping the photograph tighter. He glanced at the stacks of envelopes, the written fragments of his grandparents' lives staring back at him, waiting to be uncovered.

Devon unfolded the letter and began to read.

July 15, 1941
Somewhere in Europe

Mi amor,
The days are long, but the nights are worse. I close my eyes, and for a few seconds, I pretend I'm back home — pretend I can hear your laughter in the kitchen, pretend I can smell your arroz con pollo on the stove. But when I wake, it's nothing but the cold and the waiting.

I won't lie to you. It's harder than I thought, and I don't know how much longer I can carry the weight of it. Some days, I think about the things I did before I met you, before I found something worth fighting for. Before you taught me what love was supposed to look like.

I still remember the night you told me, "Dios tiene un plan para todos, even the ones who lost their way." I wanted to believe you. I want to believe you still.

I write to you because it's the only thing keeping me steady. The thought that somewhere out there, you're praying for me. I don't deserve those prayers, but I hold on to them, anyway.

One day, when this is over, I promise I'll take you West like we always dreamed — some place where we can build something that lasts, some place where I can finally be the man you believe I am.

Until then, keep praying. I think that's the only reason I'm still standing.

Siempre,
Dalton

Tres sat back on his heels, gripping the letter in his hands. Dalton Sr.'s words echoed in his mind, settling deep in his chest in a way he hadn't expected.

It wasn't just the war. It wasn't just the loneliness of being overseas.

It was the weight of regret. The quiet confession of a man who carried more in his heart than Tres had ever known.

He had always believed his grandparents' story started when they arrived in Arizona in 1952. They built Vargas Ranch, raised Padre, and kept faith at the center of their lives. That was the only version of them he had pictured.

But this letter? It didn't sound like a man who had everything figured out. It didn't sound like the solid foundation Tres had always imagined.

He swallowed hard, rubbing his thumb over the faded ink. "Padre never talked about this," he murmured.

Devon glanced at him, brow furrowed. "You really didn't know?"

Tres shook his head. "I knew about Vargas Ranch. Knew about how faith shaped their lives. But this—this is different."

He looked back down at the words.

"Before you taught me what love was supposed to look like."

"Before you told me Dios tiene un plan, even for the ones who lost their way."

Tres had spent his whole life believing Dalton Sr. had always been strong, unwavering, steady in faith. But here, on this tattered piece of history, was a man admitting he had been lost before Maria found him.

He exhaled slowly, staring at the pile of letters in front of them. How much more did they not know?

He glanced at Devon, the questions already forming. "We need to keep reading."

This wasn't just history anymore. It was personal.

2

DEVON FLIPPED THROUGH another stack of yellowed envelopes, the weight of history pressing against his fingertips. The storage room smelled of old paper, dust, and faint traces of cedar — probably from the wooden boxes that had been sitting untouched for decades.

He glanced at Papi, who was still holding Dalton Sr.'s letter, staring at it like it held answers he hadn't known he was looking for.

"We should organize these," Devon said, breaking the silence. "See if there's a full conversation here."

Papi set the letter down carefully and nodded. "Yeah. Otherwise, we're just picking pieces out of the dark."

Devon pulled another envelope from the pile, eyes flicking over the faded ink. His breath hitched. September 10, 1941.

"This one's from Maria."

Papi's gaze snapped to him. "Let me see."

Devon unfolded the letter carefully, eyes tracing the delicate script, before he began to read aloud.

September 10, 1941

Mi querido,

I forgot to take off the ring this morning. I realized it too late — just as Luis was readying the horses for the field. He saw it, I know he did. He didn't say anything, but the way his eyes lingered... I am afraid. If he tells Papi, what will I do?

I should not be writing this. I should be praying instead, asking God to quiet my restless heart.

I was reading this morning and found something I think will speak to you:

"With regard to the works of man, by the word of your lips I have avoided the ways of the violent. My steps have held fast to your paths; my feet have not slipped." Psalm 17:4-5

You have avoided the ways of the violent, mi amor. I know sometimes you still wrestle with the past, with the weight of choices you wish you could undo. But you stand on a new path now, one that God has laid before you. Your feet have not slipped. They will not slip, so long as you hold fast to Him.

This is why I love you. Not because you are perfect, but because you have chosen something greater than yourself. I see it in your words, in the way you speak of our future, in the way you hold on to hope.

I will wait for you, siempre.

Maria

Devon lowered the letter slowly, the silence between him and Papi stretching longer than he expected.

Papi shook his head, his jaw tightening. "She was married to him before the war." His voice was quiet, measured, but Devon could hear the undercurrent of realization beneath it.

Devon ran a hand over his face. "And hiding it from her father."

Papi exhaled sharply and stood, running a hand through his hair. "I don't—" He cut himself off, turning away for a long moment.

Devon watched him, watched the way his father wrestled with something deeper than just a revelation.

Papi had always spoken about Dalton Sr. and Maria with certainty—as if their faith had always been strong, their life had always been steady. But now? There were cracks. Undiscovered history Papi hadn't even known to look for.

Devon glanced back at the pile of letters. "There's more. We need to keep reading."

Papi hesitated. Then, slowly, he nodded. "Yeah. We do."

Devon wiped the sweat from his brow with the back of his hand. The storage shed was stifling, the thick summer air pressing against his skin like a weighted blanket. Even with the doors cracked open, the heat wrapped around them, suffocating and relentless.

Papi rolled his shoulders, exhaling sharply. "We should take these inside."

Devon nodded, already feeling the sweat gathering at the back of his neck. "Yeah. If we stay out here much longer, we'll be reading history from heaven."

Papi huffed a laugh and grabbed a crate. Devon stacked a few smaller boxes, hefting them toward the door. As he reached for the last one, something shifted beneath the pile—a leather-bound journal, its edges worn with time, tucked beneath a folder of loose papers.

"Wait."

Papi paused, looking back.

Devon pulled the journal free, running his fingers over the cracked leather. It wasn't a ledger, wasn't part of the ranch records. When he flipped it open, he froze.

Maria Vargas.

Her name was scrawled across the first page in neat, looping script.

Papi stepped closer, his brows knitting together. "Is that...?"

Devon nodded, pulse kicking up. "Her journal."

They had found the letters. But this—this was her private words, her own story beyond what she had shared with Dalton Sr.

Papi stared at it, silent.

Devon swallowed hard, feeling the weight of the discovery settling between them. They had been searching for history. Now, they were holding it.

Devon tucked Maria's journal under his arm and stacked a few more envelopes into the nearest crate. The storage shed felt like an oven, and his shirt clung uncomfortably to his back as he and Papi lugged the boxes toward the ranch house.

By the time they made it inside, the cool air felt like an answered prayer. Papi set his crate down by the dining table, rubbing his neck. "We should go through them in order," he muttered, eyeing the stacks of letters with a look Devon recognized — his father wasn't just looking at history anymore. He was seeing his grandparents differently.

Devon had just pulled out a chair when his phone buzzed.

Raina: *How much longer?*

He exhaled, running a hand through his sweat-damp hair. He'd lost track of time.

"Raina wants to know when I'll be home," he said, shooting Papi a knowing look.

Papi didn't answer. His attention was locked onto a small slip of folded paper tucked between the envelopes they'd just stacked. Not a letter. Not Maria's handwriting.

Papi slowly picked it up, brows furrowing deeper with each second.

Devon caught the tension in his father's shoulders. "What is it?"

Papi turned the note over, his jaw tightening as he read. "Enzo Ricci — "

The ink was faded, but the name was clear.

Devon's pulse kicked up.

Ricci?

That wasn't their grandfather's name.

TRES LAY FLAT on his back, staring at the ceiling, listening to the quiet hum of the house settling in for the night. The bedroom was dark except for the soft glow of the moon filtering through the curtains, casting shadows across the walls.

But he wasn't asleep.

He had tried—closing his eyes, willing his mind to slow—but Enzo Ricci wouldn't leave him alone.

Tres let out a long, slow exhale.

Next to him, Catalina rolled over. "Ay, Tres. You sound like the weight of the whole world is on you," she murmured, voice thick with sleep but laced with concern.

He hesitated before answering. "Yeah."

A pause. Then the rustling of sheets as she turned toward him. "*Qué pasó?* You've been like this all evening."

Tres ran a hand over his face, debating how much to say. But he knew better—Catalina could always tell when something was heavy on his mind. He wasn't fooling her.

"Devon and I found something today," he admitted finally. "In the storage shed. Old letters from my grandparents."

She hummed softly. "Mm. And now you're losing sleep over history?"

He exhaled again. He turned, meeting her gaze in the dim light. "I don't think Dalton Sr. was his real name."

Catalina blinked. "*Qué?*"

Tres pushed himself up slightly, resting against the headboard. "One of the papers—it wasn't Maria's handwriting, wasn't part of the letters. But it had a name." He swallowed. "Enzo Ricci."

She sat up beside him; the sheets pooling around her waist. "That's Italian."

"It is."

She frowned, searching his face. "Your *abuelo* was out here living a whole other life?"

Tres shook his head slowly. "I don't know yet. But I think Maria knew. And Padre didn't."

Catalina absorbed that for a long moment, quiet. Then, carefully, she reached for his hand, squeezing gently. "*Ay, amor.* If this is the truth, are you ready for it?"

Tres let out a slow breath, feeling the weight of it settle deeper.

"I don't know," he admitted. "But I don't think I can leave it alone now."

Catalina pressed her lips together thoughtfully, then leaned into him, resting her head against his shoulder.

"Then, we find out," she said softly. "Together, no?"

Tres stared into the dim room, feeling the uncertainty gnawing at his chest. He wasn't sure what finding out the truth would mean, but one thing was certain.

Dalton Vargas wasn't born. He was made.

The thought settled deep, anchoring itself in the quiet of the night.

The house had fallen still, the rhythmic creaks of settling wood the only sound filling the space. Catalina's breathing evened out beside him, her warmth grounding him, but sleep didn't come.

He turned the name Enzo Ricci over in his mind, again and again, trying to make sense of it. Of Maria's words. Of Padre's legacy.

What had his grandfather done?

What had he been running from?

Outside, the first hints of dawn crept in, streaking soft gold across the walls.

Tres exhaled, shifting onto his back, eyes fixed on the ceiling. He hadn't gotten a single hour of rest.

By the time Devon entered the ranch house, the sun was already high, but there was tension in his posture.

"You still thinking about it?"

Tres nodded, pushing himself away from the kitchen counter. He led his son back to the dining table, where the boxes sat untouched since last night.

Devon settled into a chair, tapping a finger against Maria's journal. "You ready to figure out what she knew?"

Tres ran a hand down his face, weary but resolute. He wasn't sure what he expected when Devon opened the pages. But when his son started reading, he knew one thing for sure—his grandparents' story was nothing like he'd thought.

Tres exhaled, slowly and measured, like he could force the tension out with his breath. He had spent his entire life believing in the Vargas legacy—in the faith, the hard work, the steady presence of the generations before him. But now, in one slip of paper, that certainty had cracked.

Devon drummed his fingers against the table. "It could be nothing. Maybe it's just an old name. People change names sometimes."

Tres shook his head. His gut told him otherwise. "No. If it was nothing, why did he never tell Padre?"

Devon hesitated. Tres could see the subtle change in his son's expression—excitement at the discovery, but also understanding of the weight it carried for Tres.

Tres's fingers hovered over Maria's journal, the weight of it almost unbearable. "If anyone knew the truth, it was her." He didn't open it right away. Did he want to know?

Devon nudged the book toward him. "Papi, if you don't read it, I will."

Tres exhaled, then finally flipped open the first page. The script was elegant, deliberate, and for a second, Tres could almost hear Maria's voice in his mind—the quiet wisdom, the strength she carried, the faith she held onto so fiercely.

They scanned the pages quickly, eyes catching fragments of daily routines, prayers, private thoughts about the ranch. But then Tres' fingers froze on a passage, skimming it once before reading aloud.

"I don't know if he'll ever stop running."

Tres stiffened. Devon jotted notes in a notepad.

"Every time I say his name, I see something flicker in his eyes. Not about his new name. The one he left behind."

Tres exchanged a glance with Devon, heart pounding harder now.

"One day, I hope he'll tell me everything."

Devon leaned back, exhaling. "She knew."

Tres swallowed hard, nodding slowly. "And she never told anyone."

Silence stretched between them, thick with the weight of revelation. Tres turned the journal pages slowly, flipping back through the entries they'd skimmed, searching for something—anything—that would make sense of the name sitting between them.

Devon drummed his fingers against the table, deep in thought. Then, suddenly, his fingers froze, his expression shifting.

Tres caught the change. "What?"

Devon pulled the first letter from yesterday off the stack, smoothing out the creases with deliberate care. Dalton Sr.'s letter.

His voice was steady when he read the line aloud.

"Before you told me... even for the ones who lost their way."

Tres's heartbeat kicked up.

Devon looked at him sharply. "We thought he was just talking about the war. But what if—" He glanced back at the journal, then at the name scrawled on the slip of paper. Enzo Ricci.

Tres exhaled slowly.

Lost.

Dalton Sr.—Enzo Ricci?—had been lost before Maria found him.

He hadn't just left behind a place. He left behind a name. A past. A whole life.

Tres stared at the paper again, the truth settling deeper in his chest.

Dalton Vargas wasn't just created.

He was reinvented.

3

———

DEVON SAT AT the dining table, tapping his fingers against the wood, eyes skimming over Maria's journal again. The whole thing itched at the back of his mind, like an answer was right there, just barely out of reach.

Papi was quiet, elbows resting on the worn tabletop, studying the slip of paper that had rattled everything they thought they knew. His brow was furrowed, his grip tight around the edge of the document.

The name stared back at them.

Enzo Ricci.

Not Dalton Vargas.

Not the man Papi had believed was the foundation of the family's legacy.

"You ever really thought about why Padre was so passionate about helping ex-cons?" Devon asked, voice measured, careful.

Papi blinked, shifting his attention. "What?"

Devon leaned forward, resting his forearms against the table. "Padre spent his whole life giving men second chances—ranch hands, former inmates, guys no one else wanted to take a risk on. And Maria's letter—it wasn't just about the war. She wrote, 'You have avoided the ways of the violent, *mi amor*... You still wrestle with the past, with choices you wish you could undo.'"

Papi's jaw tightened, his posture shifting slightly, but he

stayed silent.

Devon pressed on. "What if he wasn't just running from a name? What if he was running from a crime?"

The weight of those words hung between them, thick and unmoving.

Papi pressed his lips into a tight line, staring hard at the paper in front of him. He let out a slow breath, but there was no immediate rebuttal—only silence.

"You think he was a criminal?" Papi finally asked, voice low, deliberate.

Devon exhaled. "I think he might have been involved in something. Something bad enough that he thought changing his name was his only way out."

Papi shook his head slowly, rubbing his hand down his face. "No," he muttered. "Padre would have never stood for it if he thought his own father was a criminal."

"Maybe Padre didn't know," Devon countered.

Papi ran a hand through his hair, tension evident in the way his shoulders squared. "If he had any inkling, it had to be something less black-and-white. Maybe he wasn't a criminal—maybe he was a man trying to outrun something he couldn't fix."

Devon studied him. Papi looked conflicted, like admitting the possibility felt like a betrayal.

"Padre said men deserved a second chance," Papi said, voice quiet but firm. "Not because they were innocent, but because grace demanded it."

Devon sat back. "And maybe that belief started with Enzo Ricci and Maria."

Papi let out a sharp breath, shaking his head. "This whole thing is messier than I ever imagined." He shifted, like trying to physically shake off the unease. Then, after a beat, Devon saw the gears turning in his father's mind.

"You know..." Papi dragged a hand down his face. "Sawyer came here years ago—you remember him? I hired him. But Padre mentored him. He never stopped believing men could change."

Devon picked up the thread. "And Chef—he never uses his real name. Is that why?"

Papi blinked, letting out a short breath—not quite laughter, more like reluctant realization.

"Nobody knows," he admitted. "Padre always said names don't matter, only the work a man does with his second chance."

Devon raised an eyebrow. "That sound familiar?"

Silence.

Papi exhaled sharply, shaking his head, like trying to physically push the thought aside. "No. We're not getting sidetracked."

Devon didn't let up. "That's what Padre always said, right? That names don't matter—only the choices a man makes." He gestured to the slip of paper again. "But what if your grandfather didn't get a second chance the way Sawyer and Chef did? What if he took it?"

Papi hesitated. Just for a second.

Then, slowly, he nodded. "We need to figure out why he changed it. What he left behind."

TRES STOOD IN the ranch house kitchen, hands braced against the counter, staring absently at the old storage box sitting on the table.

It was too early to feel this restless.

The morning light filtered through the window, painting gold streaks across the tile floors, but it did nothing to quiet the unease rattling inside him.

He and Devon had been rifling through Maria's journal, the letters, and the box for days. All they found were more questions.

Behind him, a chair scraped against the tile.

He blinked, glancing over to see River settling at the table, balancing Marly on her lap while flipping through a notebook with one hand.

"Morning," she said, sliding the notebook aside long enough to sip her coffee.

Tres nodded, but his gaze drifted back to the box.

River studied him, then lifted a brow. "You've got that look."

Tres huffed. "What look?"

"The one you get when your head's too full to sit still."

Before he could respond, Sloane and Elena burst into the kitchen, voices overlapping as they rattled off complaints about being stuck inside.

"It's too hot to do anything," Sloane grumbled.

Elena flopped dramatically into the nearest chair. "I'm bored."

River sighed, giving Tres a pointed look before standing. "That's my cue."

Marly perked up. "Where are we going?"

River grabbed her coffee. "The stables. You all need to move around, and the horses don't complain when you talk their ears off."

The twins brightened instantly, darting toward the door with renewed excitement.

Tres shook his head, trying to pull himself back into the present.

River smirked, pausing at the threshold. "You've got a lot on your mind. Talk to Catalina." She gave him one last knowing glance before stepping out after the kids.

Tres glanced toward the hallway as his wife stepped in, plaiting her hair into a loose braid. She moved with that quiet certainty, reading the tension in his shoulders before he could even say a word.

She crossed to the counter, grabbing a mug. "You didn't sleep much."

He exhaled, rubbing his jaw. "No."

She took a slow sip, watching him. "Still thinking about your *familia*?"

A nod.

A silence stretched between them before she tilted her head slightly. "And what is the worst that you think happened?"

He huffed. "That Devon's right. That he was running from something—maybe something violent. Maybe a crime."

She considered that, then met his eyes. "And that *qué cambia?*"

His shoulders tensed, and he nodded. "Yes, it changes everything."

"Does it?"

He frowned. "Catalina—"

She set her coffee down with a soft clink. "But what if you already know the most important part?"

That made him pause.

Her gaze didn't waver. "You know how it ended. You know he built Vargas Ranch. You know he raised Padre, taught him faith, built this legacy." She gestured toward the house, the land beyond it. "Does knowing the beginning erase it all?"

His grip tightened on the counter.

"No," he admitted, barely above a whisper.

She nodded, shifting slightly closer. "Then maybe the question isn't just 'what happened?' Maybe it's 'why did he change?'"

Tres swallowed hard.

Her voice softened. "Sometimes people run because they're guilty. Sometimes they run because they're scared. And sometimes—" She held his gaze. "Sometimes they run because they want to start over."

He stared at her, everything pressing in at once.

Then, slowly, he nodded as he whispered the family motto, "We do not deviate from the Lord's plan."

"Ay. Words from Dalton and Maria. A couple grounded in faith."

"Words to build the foundations of a faith-filled legacy," he said.

Catalina gave a small nod, studying his face for another quiet moment before offering a knowing smile. "Your *abuelo* carried those words in his heart. And now, so do you."

She squeezed his hand once, letting the words settle between them. Then, finally, she let out a small breath, rolling her shoulders like shaking off the weight of something heavy.

"Enough of this serious talk." Her lips curved into something softer. "Cookies don't bake themselves, no?"

Tres chuckled as he picked up the box and settled in the dining room, more at peace, but still longing for answers.

4

THE AFTERNOON SUN slanted through the dining room window, casting long shadows across the table littered with old papers, family records, and his open laptop. Devon leaned back in his chair, absently rubbing his neck, the screen glowing in front of him.

The spicy aroma of Mami's enchiladas drifted from the kitchen, thick with melted cheese and roasted chicken. His stomach growled—loud enough that Papi smirked from across the table.

"You should eat," Papi muttered, sorting through the latest stack of documents, still stubbornly focused.

Devon huffed. "You should too."

But neither moved, both caught between the pull of their search and the unspoken anticipation of what they might find.

Through the doorway, River's voice floated in from the kitchen, mingling with the clatter of dishes and bursts of laughter from the kids. The ranch house had always been full of sound—comforting, familiar, grounding—even in moments like this, when Devon felt like the past was knocking on his door.

"Dinner's ready!" Mami's call cut through the hum of conversation.

Papi sighed, shutting a folder with a decisive thump. "Time-out for food?"

Devon exhaled, stretching his arms. "Like Mami would give us a choice."

The kitchen was full, the smaller table packed tight with overlapping voices and the sharp scrape of serving spoons against dishes. Devon settled into a spot in the corner, shifting slightly to make room for Marly, who had wedged herself between River and Elena. He fired off a text to his wife to eat without him.

The air was thick with the scent of Mami's enchiladas, the smoky depth of roasted chilies mingling with the rich melted cheese bubbling at the edges of each tortilla. Devon took his first bite, and the warmth spread over his tongue — the perfect balance of spice and savory depth, the kind of meal that lingered long after the last bite.

"Nothing beats Catalina's cooking," River murmured, reaching for her glass of tea. "She could teach a masterclass on enchiladas alone."

Mami waved her off with a soft laugh, shaking her head as she passed the tray for seconds.

Devon was just about to load another serving onto his plate when River glanced his way. "So, how's the family history project going?"

He slowed his movement, setting his fork down instead.

Papi barely lifted his head.

Dalton chewed absently, focused more on his plate than the conversation.

Marly kicked her feet under the table, watching Devon expectantly — waiting for an answer just like River was.

"It's... interesting," Devon said carefully, trying not to shift in his seat.

River lifted a brow. "That's vague."

Elena leaned in. "Did you find anything straight-up wild?"

Devon cleared his throat, stealing a quick glance at Papi. "We found some letters from Maria." He turned to Marly. "Your great-great-grandmother."

"Is she your *abuela*?" Elena asked Mami.

"No, *mi amor*, Maria is your *tatarabuela*, your *abuelo's abuela*."

Her cute blue eyes rounded before she nudged her twin.

Sloane blurted out, "That's, like, prehistoric!"

Devon smiled, waiting for the family's laughter to die down.

"She wrote a lot about those early years in Texas. How she met Dalton Sr. What the ranch life was like back then."

Papi's grip on his fork tightened slightly.

Devon noticed but kept his expression neutral.

Dalton finally glanced up. "You found old letters from *Bisabuela*?"

Devon nodded, keeping his tone even. "Yeah. She talked a lot about faith. About wanting a family. And about building something that lasted."

Papi exhaled quietly, reaching for his glass, his movements a little too measured—like he was picking his way through a conversation he wasn't ready to have.

Devon could feel the tension radiating from him, but River, sensing the shift, steered the topic toward something lighter, asking Marly about her pony riding lessons.

The conversation moved on, the laughter returned, and the food was passed around again, but Devon couldn't shake it—that fleeting tightness in Papi's jaw, the way he'd pressed his lips together for just a second before focusing elsewhere.

He knew it wasn't just about Maria's letters.

It was about the name they hadn't spoken aloud.

The plates were cleared, the chatter fading into the rhythm of evening chores, but Devon was back in the dining room before anyone else, laptop open, fingers hovering over the keyboard.

Dalton J. Vargas.

He had filled in dates, locations, milestones, but the early years between his birth and 1939 remained blank. Prior to his birth were details the software filled in, showing the Vargas family came over in the late 1800s. But nothing about Dalton after that.

With a slow breath, he typed the name that had surfaced from the scrap of paper they found early on.

His fingers hovered over the keyboard, the name lingering in his mind, pressing against some unseen edge of understanding.

Enzo Ricci.

He hit enter.

The system lagged—just a second, but enough for the weight of the moment to settle deeper into his chest.

The screen blinked once, refreshed.

A name.

A timeline.

A birthdate that matched Dalton's.

A piece of history they weren't supposed to find.

His breath came slowly, measured. Too measured.

Papi's voice broke the silence behind him. "You find something?"

Devon swallowed. "Yeah. And I don't think you're gonna like it."

THE DINING ROOM had darkened since supper, shadows stretching longer as the sun dipped below the horizon. Tres stood stiffly beside Devon, looking at the laptop. He barely breathed, his hands flexing at his sides as the screen burned the truth into his mind—Enzo Ricci.

He exhaled, shaking his head. "It shouldn't be there," he murmured.

Devon turned the screen toward him. "But it is."

Tres leaned forward, scanning the name—the timeline—the suggestion loaded in the system.

Enzo Ricci.

His pulse ticked up.

That name wasn't Vargas. It wasn't family. It didn't belong in their tree.

Except—somewhere, somehow—it did.

His stomach tightened, memories scrolling in his mind, fragmented thoughts of Padre's stories, of Maria's quiet strength, of Dalton Vargas's unwavering faith.

But faith didn't rewrite history.

Tres dragged a hand down his face. "How sure are we?"

Devon pointed at the screen. "It's not a coincidence. The timelines match. The records match. And from the hints we've already found in Maria's journal."

Tres sat back, the weight pressing heavier now. He'd spent the last few days sifting through Maria's words, looking for truths written between lines of old ink, but now—now he needed something concrete.

He pushed back from the table, standing abruptly. "I need to check something."

Tres walked into the study, flipping the desk lamp on, casting light over the stacked papers and folders spread across the worn wooden desk.

He had already seen the scrap of paper with Enzo Ricci's name written in bold, uneven strokes. He and Devon had found it days ago, buried among Maria's things.

But something had nagged at him ever since.

Now, staring at it under the glow of the desk lamp, the realization hit hard.

It wasn't Maria's handwriting.

It was Padre's.

His breath stilled.

Padre had written this name down himself.

Had he known? Had he suspected?

And if he had—why had he never spoken about it?

Tres clenched his jaw, staring at the slip of paper in his hand. Maria had kept Dalton's past quiet—protected him.

Padre had searched for it—chased the truth, even if he never spoke of it.

Somewhere between the two, a choice had been made.

The thought churned in his chest, uneasy, unresolved.

Slowly, almost reluctantly, Tres reached for the stack of old papers, searching for something more—something tangible that might fill in the gaps.

He sifted through the folders until he found the one he was looking for—a letter written in early 1945, months before Dalton returned from overseas.

The words were warm, familiar, filled with longing. But one sentence stopped him cold.

"Dalton, I pray every night that the war won't take you the way New York almost did. I pray that when you come home, who you used to be will finally rest, and you will only be the man I know, so we can build our new life together."

Tres let out a slow breath, the words burning in his mind.

Maria had never forgotten who her husband was before he became Dalton Vargas.

She had simply chosen to love the man he became.

He set the letter aside, but his fingers lingered on the aging paper.

Between Maria's quiet acceptance and Padre's silent search, there was a truth here—buried deep, waiting to be unearthed.

And now, Tres had no choice but to keep digging.

5

THE BEDROOM WAS dim, bathed in the soft glow of the bedside lamp. Tres sat on the edge of the bed, absently rubbing his palms together, the rough calluses catching against each other. The steady hum of the air conditioner filled the quiet, cooling the room but doing little to ease the tension knotting in Tres's chest. A faint scent of dust and sunbaked earth clung to the air, seeping in from the ranch, a reminder of the relentless summer heat outside. But it did nothing to settle the ache twisting in his chest.

Catalina pulled back the covers, settling onto her side with practiced ease, her gray-streaked hair tumbling over one shoulder as she reached for the lotion on the nightstand. The soft scent of vanilla drifted between them as she worked it into her hands.

Tres exhaled sharply, staring at the floor. "It's true. Enzo Ricci. That's who Dalton really was."

Catalina paused, looking at him—not startled, not questioning. Waiting.

He ran a hand over his jaw, feeling the tightness there. "We found more proof." He glanced at her, voice raw. "And I think Padre knew."

Her fingers stilled against her palm, and for a moment, neither spoke.

"Tres…" The way she said his name was careful, measured—like she knew exactly where his mind was headed.

He swallowed hard. "Our whole legacy... built on lies."

It was the thought he couldn't outrun—the one clawing at the edges of his mind ever since Devon typed *Enzo Ricci* into the family tree software. The ranch, the name, the stories they had been raised on—it all felt different now. Not destroyed, but gutted, as if the roots of his family's legacy had been yanked from the earth, leaving him standing in the empty space where trust once grew.

Catalina's voice came quiet but steady. "Lies, or secrets?"

Tres's head snapped up. "What's the difference?"

She turned slightly, looking him full in the face, her expression unreadable. "You tell me."

His jaw clenched.

"You kept secrets too," she continued, voice still calm. "Like not telling Derin about his twin. Like letting Devon and Drake grow up calling us Mami and Papi, knowing we were really their aunt and uncle. You hid things to protect them, didn't you?"

The words hit deep—deeper than he wanted to admit.

He sucked in a breath, pressing his thumb into his palm. "That's not the same."

She didn't flinch. "Isn't it?"

Tres exhaled slowly, his throat tight. He had told himself those choices were for their sake—to spare them from hurt, from truths they wouldn't understand.

But Maria and Dalton...

They hadn't just hidden an uncomfortable truth. They had rewritten history.

His thoughts tangled, knotted together like barbed wire he couldn't pull apart.

But before he could form the words, Catalina spoke again.

"You decided we'd hide those things from our *muchachos*. For them. For us."

She reached out and held his hand between hers, like so

many, many times over their long marriage.

"What if they did it for the same reason?"

Her shoulders rose and fell with her gentle sigh, while Tres's shoulders bunched.

"*Mi vida*, what if Dalton had to change his identity — to protect himself, to protect Maria, to keep their *familia* safe? What would you have done in his place?"

Tres stared at her, the weight of her words settling deeper than he expected. His instinct was to push back, to cling to the frustration, but her touch was steady — anchoring him. She wasn't defending Dalton. She was reminding him of choices he understood far too well.

Dalton hadn't been just a man running from his past.

He had been a man trying to build something new.

Tres blew out a slow breath, his shoulders lowering just slightly. The answers weren't simple. Maybe they never would be. But for the first time since discovering *Enzo Ricci*, he didn't feel as wrecked.

Just… changed.

As he reached over to turn off the bedside light, his wife spoke.

"I think I'll ask River to make her lasagna for dinner tomorrow, no? Honor your Italian heritage."

Tres chuckled, grateful for the way his sweet wife lifted his mood.

THE BEDROOM WAS cool, the steady hum of the air conditioner drowning out the distant chirp of crickets outside. Devon kicked off his boots by the door, stretching his shoulders as he set Maria's worn leather-bound journal on the nightstand.

Raina emerged from Cliff's room, her curls slightly tousled, the soft glow from the hallway catching in the lighter strands. She pressed a gentle kiss to Devon's cheek.

"He's asleep," she murmured, her voice quiet but warm.

Devon nodded, but guilt pinched at the edges of his thoughts. He should have been the one to tuck Cliff in, whisper *dulces sueños* against his son's forehead, feel the tiny weight of his hand clutching his shirt.

Raina caught the look before he even spoke.

"One missed 'sweet dreams' won't ruin him," she assured, resting a palm lightly against his chest. "You're here. He knows that."

She always knew how to settle him, steady him — just like she had from the moment they started building their life together.

They climbed into bed, settling into the familiar rhythm of nighttime.

Raina sank into the pillows, stretching out with an exhale. "So, tell me. What did you and Papi find today?"

Devon hesitated for a beat, then ran a hand over his face. "Dalton wasn't always Dalton. He was… Enzo Ricci."

Raina blinked.

"Enzo Ricci," she repeated, as if tasting the name, weighing its unfamiliarity.

He nodded. "It's more than just a suspicion now. We found proof."

Raina listened carefully, her fingers smoothing over the blanket absently. He knew what she was thinking — this legacy, this family, it had always been so deeply rooted in identity. And family mattered to her in a way most people would never fully understand.

She had been an orphan once. A person without a past. So now, every name, every connection, meant something.

He didn't know what else to say — not yet. So instead, he sighed. "Mind if I read for a bit?"

Raina gave a sleepy chuckle, rolling onto her side. "Why should tonight be different? Go ahead."

She turned off the lamp, leaving Devon in the dim glow

of his book light.

He adjusted the pillows behind him, shifting Maria's journal onto his lap, running his fingers over the worn spine.

The ink had faded in places, but the words held their strength.

Papi only took a few days to get over the shock of my surprise marriage to Dalton. He had seen how diligently I wrote to him during the war, how I had pressed a kiss to the envelope before sending it off. I think, in his heart, he already knew.

Devon rubbed his thumb and index finger over his eyes. More confirmation that his *bisabuela* married Dalton in secret before the war. Not so different from many couples who did the same—some never experiencing a happy reunion like they had.

Some day, he would read the journal cover to cover, but for now, he scanned ahead, flipping carefully through the pages. Hoping some detail would jump off the page at him. His eyes snagged on a sweet sentiment.

Waking up beside my husband in our cabin feels right. Feels like home. Dalton touched my wedding band this morning, running his thumb over it like he was memorizing the weight of it on my finger.

A peace wove through him as he glanced over at Raina's sleeping form. Love for her swelled his chest. Dalton must have felt the same about Maria. The connection somehow made them seem more real to him.

But it did little to help him solve his great-grandfather's mystery.

Devon frowned slightly, flipping further, searching for something deeper—for the truth of what made Dalton change his name, bury his past.

And then—

He told me something today. Something awful. Said he had seen something—witnessed it. That's why he was released after only a few years. He made a deal to testify.

Devon stilled.

Testify.

So Dalton had seen something. Something so bad, he bargained with it.

The words sank into his gut, heavy, suffocating.

This wasn't just a name change. This wasn't just a man running from his past.

Dalton had been forced to choose—a deal made in exchange for freedom, for survival.

Devon's pulse ticked up as his mind reeled. Had he witnessed a murder? Betrayed men who once called him brother? Had it followed him all the way to Texas, buried beneath the ranch, beneath the name Vargas?

He ran a hand down his face, tension burning through his shoulders. Whatever Dalton had seen, whatever he'd traded for his release—it had been life-altering.

And now, decades later, Devon was staring at the proof.

Maria had known. Padre must have suspected.

But no one spoke of it.

They built a life in silence. On survival.

The pages crinkled slightly as he turned them, urgency replacing hesitation—but nothing immediately followed. No answer. No detail. Just Maria's quiet understanding.

A rustle beside him.

Raina stirred, shifting onto her other side, barely awake. A few stray curls settled across her cheek, brushing the pillow as she sighed.

"Still reading?" she asked, voice thick with sleep. "It's well after midnight."

Devon glanced at his watch—she was right.

But he couldn't shake it—the lingering questions, the unsettled truth buried in these pages.

He thumbed the worn edge of the journal, exhaling slowly, pressing back into the pillows.

There was more to uncover.

Much more.

6

THE MORNING HEAT seeped through the window panes, even though the air conditioner hummed steadily, doing its best to keep the Arizona summer at bay. Devon stirred, feeling the familiar weight of exhaustion pressing against his skull. Too many late nights chasing ghosts.

A gentle nudge against his shoulder.

"Dev, wake up," Raina murmured, her curls brushing against his arm as she leaned over him. "You're on dad duty while I run errands."

He groaned, rubbing his scruffy face before rolling onto his back. "Five more minutes."

She laughed, shaking her head. "Fine. But I'm leaving soon."

He sighed, forcing himself up, as Raina disappeared down the hall.

With Maria's journal tucked under his arm, Devon padded into the kitchen, drawn immediately to the promise of caffeine. The scent of freshly brewed coffee filled the air, cutting through the lingering aroma of breakfast—syrup, butter, and the unmistakable scent of bacon cooling on a plate nearby.

He wrapped an arm around Raina's waist as she added notes to her phone. Then he dropped a kiss onto that soft spot of her neck before whispering, "Thanks for making me breakfast."

"Of course."

She leaned her head back against his shoulder and he savored the too brief contact. Too soon, she twirled out of his hold, dropping her phone in her purse.

Felipa sat at the kitchen island, phone in one hand,

spoon in the other, absentmindedly pushing soggy cereal around her bowl between rapid texts. Typical sixteen-year-old.

"Can I ride my horse with Jet and Zack?" she asked, barely looking up.

Devon grabbed his coffee, taking a long, restorative sip. "Yeah, just make sure you check in with me. And let me know if I need to pick you up."

"If you got me a car, I wouldn't have to bug you."

Devon snorted. Like he felt even a little comfortable with that thought.

Felipa nodded, already halfway through another message.

Cliff climbed onto the chair at the table, a waffle gripped in his tiny hands, dark curls sticking up at odd angles from sleep.

Raina kissed Devon lightly before grabbing her keys. "I'll be back by lunch. Don't let him con you into too many movies."

"Mom, wait!" Felipa snagged her boots and followed Raina out, leaving Devon alone with their son.

Devon finally sat down after making his own plate—a waffle, crispy bacon, extra syrup. Just as he took his first bite, Cliff pointed at the journal.

"Dad, what's that?"

Devon wiped his mouth, nudging the worn book toward his son. "It's your *tatarabuela's* journal. Can you say that?"

Cliff furrowed his brows, concentrating. "Tar-ta...buela?"

Devon chuckled. "Close. *Tatarabuela*. She was Abuelo's *abuela*. Do you remember what Abuelo means?"

"Grandpa!" Cliff grinned, proud of himself.

The small victory made Devon smile. Teaching him English and Spanish was a slow process, but moments like this reminded him why he did it. Having an older sister fluent in Spanish helped.

"Want to watch a movie?" Cliff asked.

Devon nodded, rinsing his plate before setting up the TV for his son.

With Cliff occupied, Devon spread out Maria's journal and his notes, flipping open his laptop. He typed: New York. 1920s. Prison records. Enzo Ricci.

The first searches flooded with unrelated results. Too many names. Too many dead ends.

Then, buried beneath archived news articles, something caught his eye—a snippet mentioning a Ricci involved in an Italian gang.

Devon's pulse ticked up as he clicked on the link.

"Ricci testified in a high-profile murder trial, securing a plea deal for reduced sentencing."

Testified.

Just like Maria had written.

Devon sat back, heart thudding slightly. This was it—a piece of Dalton's past, rising from the shadows.

He grabbed a pen, jotting notes, flipping between articles—searching for more, for anything that told him what Dalton had seen, what he had traded for his freedom.

Just as he scrawled down the last detail, Cliff's voice rang out from the great room.

"*Abuelo*! Daddy is reading a book about my tartar sauce *abuela*!"

Devon laughed under his breath, shaking his head. "*Tatarabuela*, buddy."

Papi stepped into the kitchen, quirking a brow at Cliff. "Tartar sauce, huh?"

Cliff grinned. "Close enough."

Papi sighed, nudging the door closed before setting down a battered cardboard box on the table.

Dust lifted off the surface, swirling lazily in the kitchen light before settling. The edges were frayed, corners softened from years of being shuffled, stacked, forgotten. A faint smell of aged paper and ink curled into the air—history waiting to be unearthed.

Devon's fingers twitched against his thigh, anticipation coiling tight in his chest. He inhaled deeply, the scent stirring something restless inside him—the thrill of discovery, the rush of a puzzle about to break open.

He eyed the box, instinctively straightening. "Is that the same one?"

Papi shook his head. "Nope."

The heaviness in his father's gaze told Devon this was more than just an old collection of ranch records.

He wiped his palm against his gym shorts, as if steadying himself before reaching forward. He wasn't sure why, but the weight of the moment pressed deep.

"What did you find?"

Papi exhaled, resting a hand on the box, fingers drumming lightly against the worn cardboard. "Something that's been buried long enough."

Devon studied him, taking in the tightness around his father's mouth, the way his jaw set like he was bracing for something.

He nodded slowly, pushing his laptop aside to make space, already itching to tear into the contents.

Papi snagged a mug from the cupboard, the quiet clink of ceramic filling the space. He lifted a brow while pouring the coffee, steam curling into the air between them. "How about you shower first?"

Devon opened his mouth to protest, but after one glance at his wrinkled t-shirt, the sweat still lingering from sleep—and Papi's unwavering stare—made him exhale sharply. He scraped a hand through his hair, feeling the weight of the long night still clinging to him.

"Fine," he muttered, shoving his chair back.

Papi smirked. "I'll be here when you smell like a respectable historian."

Tres eased into the chair, sliding Devon's scribbled notebook toward him, scanning the familiar slant of his son's handwriting. *Testified in murder trial.*

The words sat heavy on the page, stark against the soft morning light pouring through the window.

He turned Devon's laptop toward him, eyes flicking across the multiple open tabs—prison records, court transcripts, old newspaper archives. Devon had been busy. This wasn't just speculation anymore. The proof was stacking up.

A tiny voice interrupted the weight settling over him.

"I'm thirsty."

Tres blinked, shaking off the heaviness coiling around him. Cliff stood at the edge of the table, dark curls tousled, green eyes glinting in the overhead lights.

He was the perfect blend of Devon and Raina—their miracle baby. The child his niece Renata had carried, the child they had waited for.

Tres pushed himself up, retrieving a juice box from the fridge, poking the tiny straw through the foil opening. Cliff watched, patiently waiting, always curious.

"Here you go, *mi pequeño*."

Cliff beamed, grabbing his drink before scurrying back toward the couch.

A muffled door creaked down the hall. The shower had stopped.

Devon emerged moments later, barefoot, hair damp, a loose t-shirt clinging slightly to his skin from lingering heat. He swiped a hand through his damp hair, tossing a glance toward the mess of papers, laptop cord, and notebooks across the kitchen table.

"Alright," he murmured, sinking into the chair across from Tres. "What did you find?"

Tres exhaled, placing a folder between them. "Prison

records. Rikers. The dates Enzo Ricci served time. And the date he left."

Devon leaned forward, fingertips pressing against the aged paper.

Tres watched his son take it in, the tight pull of his brows, the way his thumb traced the faded ink as if willing it to tell him more.

Then Tres reached into the box, pulling out something heavier. The leather notebook.

The worn edges were cracked, a deep brown that had darkened with age. Padre's handwriting peeked through the edge of the first page, sharp, deliberate, full of a young man's conflicted thoughts.

Devon's gaze sharpened. "What's this?"

Tres flipped open the cover, resting his hand lightly against the first few fragile pages. "Padre's notes and thoughts."

Devon's fingers tightened against the prison records, his eyes widening. "Padre knew?"

Tres nodded slowly. "He found out right after he turned eighteen. It wrecked him." He tapped the old pages, skimming lines that had long been burned into his memory. "Dalton had been in prison. That wasn't the worst part, though. What broke Padre was realizing he—Dalton J. Vargas—was never real."

Devon stiffened. "Padre was named after a fake identity."

Tres met his gaze, the quiet weight of generations between them pressing against the space.

Then he read part of Padre's journal aloud.

I remember a time when I was twelve. It seared into my memory because it was so odd. My abuelo on my mamacita's side lied. My papi had been out of town, and two strange men showed up. Bulky, menacing looking men. Abuelo rested a hand on my shoulder when they asked about Dalton Vargas's whereabouts. My abuelo squeezed my shoulder and told them I was Dalton. They frowned and stepped closer. My heart nearly beat out of my chest.

They asked if my papi was alive.

And that's when Abuelo lied. He said that it was just him, his daughter, and me on the ranch.

I knew what he wanted them to think — that my papi was dead — not that he was out of town buying a new bull.

Devon sat back, exhaling through his nose. Tres watched the shift in his son — saw the weight of understanding settle into his features, the same weight Tres had carried himself that morning.

It wasn't just about prison records or old headlines. It was about identity. About legacy. About the foundation their family had built — now shaken, but not broken.

A sharp vibration rattled against the counter — Devon's phone.

He swiped it, reading the text aloud. "Felipa's on her way home. Solana gave her a ride."

Tres nodded absently, flipping through the last few pages, knowing they weren't done yet.

There was still more.

Dalton's full prison records, a New York Times article detailing the murder trial — obvious proof Dalton had been in a gang, but that he had killed no one.

A list of dates — when Dalton left New York, when he arrived in Texas, when he officially became a Vargas.

Tres lifted his gaze to Devon. "No more secrets."

Devon looked back at the records, at the truths that had lived in shadows for far too long.

He nodded, slow but steady.

"No more secrets."

The past had finally unfolded across the kitchen table, piece by piece.

And now, they had to reckon with what it meant.

Tres flipped through the last few pages, knowing they weren't done yet.

Then, toward the back of the notebook, a passage stood

out—Padre's words, written with less anger, with something quieter, steadier, that came with time and maturity.

Tres exhaled, reading aloud.

It took me years to make peace with it.

I carried the weight of my name like a stone in my chest, as if I had to prove it wasn't tainted by deception.

Mamá told me I was wrong. She said my name wasn't stolen — it was redeemed.

Dalton Vargas wasn't just a disguise. He was a man pulled from the wreckage, set on solid ground, shaped by grace.

She reminded me of our verses — Psalm 17:4-5: "With regard to the works of man, by the word of your lips I have avoided the ways of the violent. My steps have held fast to your paths; my feet have not slipped." She let the words settle between us before continuing, her voice steady. "Your papi didn't avoid the ways of the violent in his youth. But he turned around. A perfect picture of what Jesus's redemptive power can do in a broken man — even one with a criminal past."

She pressed a hand to my shoulder and told me, "We do not deviate from the Lord's plan." That's what our family stood on — not the past, not the brokenness, but the transformation. What God had done through him.

It took time, but I began to see it. Not as shame. Not as betrayal. But as the story of a man saved by the grace of God for something bigger than himself.

Tres's throat tightened as he closed the notebook, the weight of those words settling between him and his son.

His nephew that he had adopted as a son and lied about it for years.

Tres exhaled slowly, gripping the worn leather cover. Padre had fought to reconcile his father's past, and now Tres felt that same battle stirring in his own chest.

The son he had raised — the boy he had claimed — he had carried that secret for so long, justifying it, protecting it. But this moment, with Devon across the table, his words steady and sure — *he forgave you years ago* — Tres felt it lift.

Like Maria had told Padre, transformation was the legacy. And that meant his own.

Suddenly, he felt a sweet peace settle over him — a healing balm for his own mistakes and for a chance to leave them at the cross.

Devon leaned forward, staring at the leather cover. "He found peace."

Tres nodded, slowly. "His mamá, Maria, helped him see it that way. See Dalton not as a liar — but as a man who had been given a second chance."

The words hung thick between him. He knew the weight they carried, especially to his fourth son.

"I forgave you years ago." Devon's whispered words soothed the ache in Tres's chest.

"I love you, son."

Devon stood and tugged him into a long, heartfelt embrace.

"I love you too, Papi."

The past wasn't just about secrets or deception anymore. It was about redemption. About the transformation that came after the wreckage — for Dalton, for Padre, and for Tres himself.

7

THE LATE AFTERNOON light streamed through the kitchen window, warm but soft, stretching golden lines across the oak table. Devon sat hunched over Maria's journal, flipping carefully through its aged pages, the ink delicate but unyielding — each word a tether to the past.

Cliff was playing with toy horses on the floor nearby, mumbling a half-English, half-Spanish story under his breath, lost in a world of his own. Somewhere down the hall, Raina hummed as she folded laundry, her voice barely audible over the murmur of the ceiling fan. And Felipa strummed on her guitar, the soft melody fitting his mood.

But Devon wasn't here — not entirely.

He was somewhere between then and now, piecing together what Maria had left behind.

Then his breath caught as he skimmed an entry, going back to read it slowly. The story behind the name of their family's mountain.

Dalton Peak. I still remember the first time I named it — spoke it aloud with certainty, as if the Lord Himself had settled it in my heart before I ever knew why.

We had been in Arizona only a few months, settling into Vargas Ranch, carving out a life in the dust and sun. My papi was with us, our son growing strong, the land stretching wide before us, promising something new — something untouched by Dalton's past.

But I knew the past still clung to him in quiet moments. I saw it in the way he would stare toward the horizon, eyes lingering on the peak, hands buried deep in his pockets, shoulders lined with tension.

So I gave the mountain his name.

"Every day," I told him, "you will look at it. And every day, you will be reminded that your name — your true name — is the beginning of a legacy. A sign of how God changed you completely, how He recharted the course of your life."

Dalton swallowed hard, eyes flickering between me and the mountain, as if weighing the truth in my words.

"You really believe that?" he asked.

"Of course, mi amor."

And just like that, the past loosened its grip.

Dalton Peak became more than a landmark. It became a testimony.

Devon stared at the words, his fingers resting lightly against the aging pages, the ink pressed deep into the parchment — a voice from the past speaking to him across time.

He swallowed, glancing up toward the window, where the afternoon light stretched long across the floorboards, soft but unwavering, just like Maria's conviction in her journal.

Dalton Peak.

It wasn't just a name — it was a declaration, a monument built from faith, from transformation, from something his great-grandmother had seen before anyone else.

Devon exhaled slowly, turning toward the sliding glass door, where the land stretched wide beyond the ranch, the peak rising against the endless Arizona sky.

Dalton had looked toward it and seen his past chasing him.

Maria had looked toward it and seen his redemption standing firm.

Devon let his eyes linger on the horizon, imagining Dalton in that moment — the weight of his mistakes pressing into his shoulders, his name spoken aloud as a promise, not as a condemnation.

How many times had Papi done the same for Devon? Seen his son's struggles, his doubts, his failures—and reminded him that his legacy wasn't just shaped by the past but by God's ability to redeem it?

He traced his thumb over the journal's edge, reverent in the quiet.

He had spent so much time digging into Dalton's secrets, peeling back layers of his past, trying to understand the man beneath the name change. But now, reading Maria's words, he saw it clearly—the name wasn't a mask. It was a second chance. A testimony sealed into the very earth they called home.

Devon pushed back from the table, standing slowly, feeling the weight of realization settle deep.

Padre had been right.

Maria had been right.

God had taken a man, a name, a life—and recharted its course, from the streets of New York to the desert of Arizona, from Ricci to Vargas, from lost to redeemed.

Devon exhaled, then reached for his phone.

He wasn't done unraveling the past—but now, he understood it differently.

TRES LEANED BACK against the worn leather couch, phone in hand, rereading Devon's text.

Discovered the full story of Dalton Peak. Heading over now.

A slow smile tugged at his lips. The final piece of their family's history, falling into place.

He set his phone down just as the deep rumble of Devon's truck echoed through the ranch yard. Moments later, the familiar sound of doors slamming shut and the excited chatter of kids signaled his arrival.

Tres stood, stretched, then crossed the room to open the front door. A gust of warm desert air rushed through the open door, carrying the familiar scent of dry earth and sage. Devon stepped through the door, Raina, Felipa, and Cliff in tow, their presence filling the space with an added warmth.

Inside the great room — the heart of the house Padre had built for his wife and mother — the family gathered. Dalton, River, their kids, Catalina, Tres — all settling into their usual spots, anticipation humming in the space between them.

Devon held Maria's journal, his expression alight with the thrill of discovery.

"Alright," he began, adjusting his stance as he held it up. "I finally know why she named it Dalton Peak."

The room quieted.

His voice was steady, reverent, as he read aloud Maria's words — the story of faith, transformation, and legacy. Clearly a talented public speaker. Tres wished he could watch him in the classroom someday.

River snorted, breaking the silence with a chuckle. "I guess it really was named after your great-grandfather, after all."

Dalton shot her a playful glare before pulling his wife closer, murmuring something soft against her ear that made her laugh.

Tres, watching Cliff weave between chairs, his toy horse clutched tight, let the warmth of the moment settle deep.

This was it. The past meeting the present, the truth finally laid bare.

He exhaled, savoring it.

River tapped a finger against her chin, studying Devon. "You should write a book about the family's history."

Devon blinked, then his entire expression lit up. "Would you help me?"

River grinned. "Of course."

Dalton cleared his throat, shifting forward. "We could

sell it in the gift shop."

Sloane, perched on the armrest of a chair, added quickly, "And online."

Tres chuckled, shaking his head. "Already thinking about marketing?"

"Well, why not?" River shrugged. "People come here for the history. Might as well give them the full story."

Dalton nodded in agreement. "Besides, if Devon's gonna write it, might as well make sure it reaches people."

Tres watched his son soak it in. Devon had spent weeks chasing the past with him—now, he had a way to preserve it.

Catalina clapped her hands together, cutting through the discussion. "We should start planning for the celebration, no?"

Tres straightened, shifting his gaze around the room. "Absolutely. The whole family will be home for it. We need to finalize the schedule."

Devon tapped Maria's journal. "I'll read the entry about Dalton Peak."

Tres nodded, firm. "And I'll close it out with some remarks."

Dalton leaned back, rubbing his jaw. "How many people do we need to accommodate again?"

Tres said, "We should invite Harley and Heidi."

Catalina smiled. "Ay, they are like *familia*."

"And the staff?" Devon asked.

"Maybe after a special meal for the family," Tres said, feeling a little selfish, wanting time with his children and grandchildren.

"Then that'd be around forty, right Mom?" Felipa asked Raina.

"I think so. Where should we host it?"

River lifted a brow. "Too bad it'll be too hot to host it near Dalton Peak itself."

Sloane hummed. "Could we do a sunrise gathering near

the mountain? Make it feel connected to its meaning."

Tres turned toward Catalina. "What do you think?"

She pursed her lips, considering. "The peak would be poetic. But too hot, no?"

Dalton nodded. "We can set up the firepit after the main talk in the dining hall—after the sun sets. Keep the storytelling going."

"I could play my guitar," Felipa offered.

"That is wonderful, *mi princesa*!" Catalina exclaimed.

The group murmured in agreement, plans shaping as the evening stretched on.

As the men finalized details, Catalina, Raina, and River moved into the kitchen, pulling ingredients from the fridge and setting out dishes. The scent of simmering spices and freshly chopped onions filled the air, mixing with the warm glow of conversation still lingering in the great room.

Tres watched as Catalina deftly pressed masa into fresh tortillas, chatting with Raina about the guest list. River stirred a pot of beans, laughing as Felipa stole a chip dipped in queso from the counter.

By the time supper was ready, the conversations had shifted into easy banter, the weight of history giving way to the simple joy of being together.

Tres stood, glancing around the room, then bowed his head, lifting his voice in prayer.

"Lord, thank You for this family, for the stories that connect us, for the legacy You have written over generations. May this celebration honor You and remind us that our steps are guided by You alone."

A quiet chorus of "Amens" followed before the family, in one voice, recited their motto:

"We do not deviate from the Lord's plan."

Tres felt it resonate deep in his chest.

Because this—this gathering, this laughter, this bond of history and faith—was exactly the plan God had set before them.

8

OCTOBER

TRES TIGHTENED his grip on the steering wheel, his fingers pressing into the leather as he and Catalina drove toward the dining hall — the only place large enough to hold their growing family. The afternoon sun poured through the windshield, baking the Arizona landscape in hues of deep gold and dusty amber.

Catalina sat beside him, her expression soft, nostalgic, as she traced the edge of her dress, lost in thought.

"It's hard to believe how much our *familia* has grown," she murmured, head turning toward the hills in the distance. "Renata, Gabe, and their little ones are finally here. I can't wait to hold Eli."

Tres hummed in agreement, though he barely heard her. His mind was elsewhere — on the history they were about to share, on the weight of it all.

"And Solana's *niña*."

He sighed.

Catalina turned to him, studying his face. "You nervous?"

Tres let out a slow breath, nodding once. "Yeah."

She reached for his hand, giving it a reassuring squeeze. "It's our story. It's our legacy. *Y es preciosa.*"

"Yeah, it *is* beautiful."

He pulled into the packed lot, rows of trucks and SUVs already filling every available space. Tres shut off the engine, resting his hands briefly on his thighs.

Catalina didn't move. Instead, she bowed her head, her voice low and sure as she clasped his hand in hers.

"Lord, settle his nerves. Give him peace in this moment. This is Your story, woven into our family's hands, guided by Your plan. Let us honor You today."

Tres exhaled, absorbing the words, then finally stepped out of the truck.

Inside, the cool rush of air conditioning was a welcome relief from the heat pressing against their backs. The hall was alive—laughter bouncing off wooden beams, voices mingling with the scent of smoked meats and barbecue sauce.

Tres and Catalina wove through the crowd, exchanging warm embraces with their children, nieces, and Diego and Katie, who had driven in from town. The energy was infectious—a celebration of family, of history, of everything Vargas Ranch stood for.

At the buffet, plates piled high with brisket, ribs, cornbread, and classic southwestern sides lined the tables, Chef ensuring everyone had more than enough.

Catalina leaned in close, her voice meant only for Tres. "We should have snuck a few Italian dishes in there."

Tres chuckled. "Next time."

Dinner stretched on in waves of conversation, but Tres barely touched the second half of his plate. He finally pushed it away and stood, his heart ticking faster as he made his way to the stage where Devon was already waiting, journal in hand.

Tres took the microphone, his voice steady as he addressed the room.

"Family—tonight, we honor the history that brought us here." He nodded to Devon, who stepped forward, opening the worn pages of Maria's journal.

The room hushed as Devon's voice filled the space, reading her words aloud—the story of why she named Dalton Peak.

As Devon spoke, Tres watched expressions shift across the crowd.

River rested a hand over her heart, eyes glistening with emotion. Dalton leaned forward, gripping his wife's hand, reverence deepening in his features. Sloane, always thoughtful, nodded slightly, absorbing every word with quiet reflection.

Madison leaned against Derin's arm. He raised it, sliding his chair closer to rest his arm around her. Years ago, Tres hadn't been sure if Derin would ever settle down. But God sent just the right woman. Watching his middle son grow into fatherhood was one of the greatest joys of his life. Derin doted on those three kids: Maverick, Bonner, and a little girl Kinsley.

Dylan and Brisa were a beautiful match. Dylan's quiet strength with her sweet spirit. Braden had thrived under the love of his adopted father and he was a doting big brother to his siblings Aubrey and Reed.

His youngest, Drake, made him so proud—well, he was proud of all his boys. His wife Candi had baked a special cake for the event and Tres looked forward to tasting it. Right now, though, little Travis squirmed in his grandpa Travis's lap while Thalen listened to the story with rapt attention.

Tres scanned the faces—generations gathered, listening about the woman who had changed their lives before any of them were ever born.

When Devon closed the journal, there was a beat of silence.

Then applause, murmurs of agreement, the warmth of understanding settling over them all.

Tres let the moment breathe, then raised the microphone once more.

He cleared his throat, steadying himself.

Then he took a steady breath, gripping the microphone as he looked out over the room—family gathered, generations seated together, faces alight with warmth and anticipation.

"Legacy."

The single word settled over them, heavy with meaning.

"It's what binds us. It's what gives us purpose. And for this family, it has always been about redemption—about stepping forward, about forging something new from the broken places."

He paused, scanning the faces before him.

"We've had our secrets." He lifted a brow, lips curving slightly as a chuckle rippled through the crowd. "And we've revealed them. And we've forgiven them."

Laughter softened, replaced by the quiet understanding that had carried them throughout generations.

"Padre—Junior—made mentoring ex-cons his life's mission. Inspired by his father's redemption story, he poured into men others had cast aside. He gave them a chance. He gave them a foundation so their feet would not slip, so they could avoid the ways of the violent."

His gaze flickered toward the back wall, where the family verses and motto proclaimed lasting truth, painted boldly for all to see.

"That's why our family verses—Psalm 17:4-5—and our motto are displayed here. It's a legacy that continues to this day."

Tres exhaled, shifting the weight of the speech toward those who had carried on the work.

"Diego and Katie—though you left the ranch, you never left the legacy. Through your feed store in town, you continue to help those in need, whether it's sharing a prayer with a patron or simply offering a hand where it's needed. Your impact is felt far beyond these fences."

His lips lifted slightly as he turned to Catalina.

"Catalina—*mi amor*—you spread wisdom and love into the lives of all who know you. And I have it on good authority that the cowboys especially love your Christmas cookie tins."

Soft laughter filled the space, Catalina shaking her head with knowing amusement.

Tres pressed forward, his voice steady.

"Dalton and River. What can I say? You are a strong leader, worthy of the name. The way you pushed your generation to expand the guest ranch and resort has gone far beyond what any of us imagined. And River—your stories share our love of Arizona, our love of God, with many who will never grace the threshold of our home."

He turned toward the next generation of leaders.

"Dylan and Brisa, Adan and Solana—the work you do with Braden's Hope brings so much joy and healing to children and veterans through the equine therapy program. You bring restoration where it's needed most."

His gaze shifted toward Derin and Madison, their presence always steady.

"And Derin and Madison—the way you change athletes' lives at the sports complex is remarkable. Whether guiding them through transitions into a new career or creating a safe place for rehab, you do it all while modeling Christ's love."

Then to Devon.

"Devon and Raina—your programs for children at the resort give them a chance to explore in ways that matter to them. And Devon—your love for preserving our family's history reminds us all why we're here today."

A beat of silence passed before Tres pressed a hand to his stomach with a grin.

"Drake and Candi—each interaction you have with our guests, whether it's foam art in their specialty coffee or a freshly baked treat," He patted his waistline, laughter rippled through the room, "you always take the time to listen, to offer a kind word to whoever needs it."

Finally, he turned toward their Montana branch of the family.

"Renata and Gabe—you are our emissaries to Montana, bringing new traditions to an entirely different set of tourists. And you do it all with grace, a smile, and Christ's love at the center."

Tres looked around the room, his voice thick with emotion, the moment settling deep.

"Each of you, whether born a Vargas or grafted into this family tree through marriage or adoption, has made a lasting impact—far beyond what Dalton Sr. could have ever envisioned." He exhaled, voice firm. "I'm proud to be a Vargas. And I'm proud of the lives each of you has impacted for good."

He extended a hand, his voice resonant.

"Join me in reciting our motto."

As one, the family recited their prayer, voices strong and sure:

"We do not deviate from the Lord's plan."

Tres closed his eyes for a brief second, letting the words settle into his chest.

Because this—this moment, this gathering, this legacy—was proof that they never had.

Behind The Scenes

———————

THE INSPIRATION FOR this novella came from a scene I wrote all the way back in book 1 *Falling for a Real Cowboy* where the brothers and cousins bring River to the dining hall for a meal with them while Tres and Catalina went out on a date.

That one scene spawned dozens of ideas about the family's history. Devon was the resident historian and shared some facts about the family. His interest in history plays a role in several books in the series.

After writing book 5, I sat down and brainstormed a possible Vargas Origins series based on the different tidbits about Maria and Dalton Sr. that I sprinkled throughout the series. The idea to tie their story to a criminal came before the first book was published. Their family verses and motto had such deep meaning and had to have equally deep roots.

I had already woven into each book a character who was impacted by the verses and motto in many different ways.

As each book unfolded in the series, it didn't seem right to give Padre (Junior) or Tres a criminal background. That left me with the founding couple.

Arizona has a long history of being a place that attracts people from all walks of life—promising second chances and redemption in the heart of the desert or high country. My own story is one of second chances, though not anywhere as extreme as Dalton Sr.'s.

Anyway, the more I thought about all the different aspects, the more it made sense to weave the history the way I did.

While this novella leans more into history than romance, the Vargas legacy continues. If you loved this glimpse into their past, I hope you'll join me for my upcoming *Love at Vargas Ranch* series, where faith and love take center stage once again.

And speaking of love — keep reading for an excerpt from *Her Honest Cowboy Twin*, the first book in the series!

Blessings,

Karen Baney

VARGAS RANCH SERIES
Love, Cowboys, and Faith-Filled Journeys

Prequel: Falling for a Fake Cowboy – Sawyer & Cara
She's rich. He's poor. One unexpected photo could unravel everything — will love be enough to stand against the past?

Book 1: Falling for a Real Cowboy – Dalton & River
She's chasing redemption. He's running from love. Can faith bridge the divide between them before it's too late?

Book 2: Falling for a Shy Cowboy – Dylan & Brisa
She's a single mom starting over. He's the quiet cowboy who's loved her from afar. Will love, faith, and courage heal their wounded hearts?

Book 3: Falling for a Bossy Cowboy – Derin & Madison
She's a sports legend at a crossroads. He's a cowboy with no filter. Can two opposites learn to trust, grow, and fight for love?

Book 4: Falling for a Smart Cowboy – Devon & Raina
She's devoted to giving orphaned children hope. He's determined to leave the ranch behind. Will buried secrets break their hearts — or bind them forever?

Book 5: Falling for a Humbug Cowboy – Drake & Candi
She's the happiest person he's ever met. He's in no mood for Christmas. Will holiday magic thaw his frosty heart before the season ends?

Book 6: Falling for a Devoted Cowgirl – Solana & Adan
They've secretly loved each other for years. He's bound by doubts. She's held back by fear. Can they finally take the leap and claim the love they've always dreamed of?

Book 7: Falling for a Pregnant Cowgirl – Renata & Gabe
She's pregnant with a child that isn't hers. He can't stop himself from falling for her. But will the truth pull them apart — or bring them closer?

Excerpt

From *Her Honest Cowboy Twin*

ALL THE STEREOTYPES about identical twins finishing each other's sentences and being besties for life — those were lies. Parker Quaid knew it firsthand.

He jammed his cell phone into his pocket, frowning so deep he could almost feel his brows touching. His twin had struck again.

"Parker!"

He turned toward the sound of his boss, Dylan Vargas' voice, cutting through the low murmur of morning activity in the barn.

"C-c-could you get Pansy and Red ready?"

"Sure thing."

Parker had been hired on at Vargas Ranch for all of two months. He liked it here. The wide-open desert. Sunrises painted in soft gold and burnt orange, stretching endlessly over the horizon. The quiet, still mornings with room for a man to think. Maybe too much room.

He ambled toward Pansy's stall, the horse whuffling softly, her breath warm as he stepped inside. The smell of hay and leather filled the air, earthy and familiar. He placed the halter carefully over her head, opened the gate, and led her down the alleyway to the grooming area, hooves clopping against the packed dirt with a steady rhythm.

Routine. He liked routine. It didn't ask questions or cast suspicion. Didn't look at him sideways like he might turn crooked any minute, just because his twin had.

He ran the brush along Pansy's coat, slow and steady, the soft scrape of bristles blending with the distant creak of a stall door swinging shut. His mind drifted to the email waiting for him from his attorney. Bad news. He already knew it—he hadn't even needed to read past the first line.

Lucas had conned an elderly widow out of thousands of dollars, promising her some fake land deal, taking her retirement savings, then vanishing. Parker barely remembered her face from back home in Flagstaff. Been years since he'd been back. Lucas, on the other hand, had gained her trust. And somehow, through forged documents and slick talking, Lucas took everything from her.

And he'd used Parker's social security number when the court ruled against him, forcing Parker to pay reparations. He snorted, the sound abrupt in the still air. Like Lucas would ever work an honest day in his life.

Parker tightened the saddle's cinch a little harder than necessary, Pansy shifting away from him, her tail flicking in irritation. He exhaled slowly, rubbing his hand along her neck in silent apology. None of this was her fault. It wasn't even entirely his own. But that hadn't mattered to his previous employer, who put more weight on the court's ruling tied to his social than the name on the judgment being different. They'd garnished his wages and sent the money to the court for distribution.

Parker quit when he found out. His attorney was still trying to straighten it all out. The email didn't look promising. He might not get a dime of it back.

The Vargases had given him a chance when no one else

would. If they saw him as just another Quaid disaster, he'd lose more than a job. He'd lose the only place that still felt like his.

The old fable about Midas? Lucas was the opposite. Everything he touched burned.

Parker led Pansy to the trail ride staging area, tying her off at the rail. The heat rising off the packed dirt smelled faintly of mesquite and sunbaked silt, a far cry from the crisp chill of Flagstaff.

Maybe Lucas hadn't finished ruining his life yet.

As Parker passed Adan Franco on the way back down the alleyway, the ranch hand tipped his hat in greeting, boots scuffing against the ground.

His mind started recounting all the ways Lucas's crimes had made his life difficult as he brushed Red's coat. Parker had been arrested no less than five times. That's how he learned odd little facts about identical twins — like that their fingerprints were different. Bless the one cop in Flagstaff who told him about it. Saved him from actually going to jail or serving prison time for his twin.

He shook his head. Didn't do him any good dwelling on things he couldn't control. His co-worker Adan would tell him not to count the offenses. Sage advice.

Parker finished readying Red before leading him out to the staging area. Dylan thanked him before giving a few parting instructions and mounting up.

He watched as the group rode away, a smile twitching at the corner of his mouth when a teenage girl squealed — something about her horse going too fast. It wasn't. Barely a walk. Clearly a novice.

Turning on his booted heel, he dragged the large barn door closed, the hinges groaning in protest. Despite it being mid-November, the temperatures were still climbing up to the low-nineties. A little unseasonably warm for the Sonoran desert. Dust swirled lazily in the air, catching in the faint breeze.

Back home, it probably would have snowed by now. Crisp, chilly air. Fresh. None of this dust-laden stuff.

He growled in frustration. He needed to pull himself out of his foul mood. Lucas only won if Parker gave in to bitterness. He knew that—but letting go wasn't easy.

Toasted Toffee was due for time in the corral, so Parker led the ranch manager's horse out for some fresh air and exercise before returning inside.

He stowed the extra tack in the dimly lit tack room, the familiar scent of saddle soap and worn leather filling the space. Then he hosed down the grooming area, listening to the steady rush of water hitting the dirt, the scent of damp earth rising around him.

Finally, he stepped into the office to check the schedule.

Only to run into the most beautiful woman. Warm chocolate brown eyes. Long brown hair.

He steadied her, her floral-scented shampoo lingering in the space between them, warmth sparking under his skin. Her rounded eyes settled for a beat or two into something almost apologetic.

Then, as if this day hadn't been bad enough, her eyes lit with fire—the kind that could scorch the earth.

"You!"

Knowing full well he'd never met the woman before in his life, Parker could only assume Lucas had struck again.

About the Author

Karen Baney is passionate about writing stories full of flawed characters. She enjoys weaving together stories of second chances, redemption, and overcoming personal trials. As a transplant to Arizona, she loves researching the state's history and finding ways to seamlessly incorporate real history and real settings into her novels. In addition to writing and speaking, Karen works as a Software Development Manager for a Christian ministry.

Her faith plays an important role both in her life and in her writing. Karen and her husband, Jim, make their home in Gilbert, Arizona, with their two dogs, Bella and Daisy. Both Jim and Karen are active at Rock Point Church in Queen Creek, Arizona.

Discover faith-laced stories with characters who feel like lifelong friends.

Visit www.karenbaney.com to discover more historical romance series set in the American West. Follow Karen's writing journey and get behind-the-scenes glimpses of her research adventures on social media.

Facebook: @AuthorKarenBaney
X: @karen_baney
Instagram: @AuthorKarenBaney
BookBub: Follow Karen Baney for new release alerts

Books By Karen Baney

<u>Contemporary Romance</u>

Vargas Ranch Series:
Love is in the air at the Vargas Guest Ranch & Resort near Wickenburg, Arizona. Meet the Vargas family—five swoon-worthy brothers and their cousins who live by their family motto: "We do not deviate from the Lord's plan." These rugged cowboys run a successful working ranch and luxury resort while navigating the rollercoaster of finding true love.

Falling for a Fake Cowboy
Falling for a Real Cowboy
Honeymoon with a Real Cowboy
Falling for a Shy Cowboy
Falling for a Bossy Cowboy
Falling for a Smart Cowboy
Falling for a Humbug Cowboy
Falling for a Devoted Cowgirl
Falling for a Pregnant Cowgirl
Falling for a Cowboy's Legacy

Steadfast Love Series:
The *Steadfast Love* series follows a close-knit group of friends as they navigate the beautiful mess of modern life in the Phoenix area—workplace drama, complicated families, and love that shows up when they least expect it. These contemporary romances blend emotional depth with authentic faith, reminding us that even when life unravels, God's love never does.

The Heart I Rescue (prequel)
The Air I Breathe

Historical Western Romance

Prescott Pioneers Series:
Step back in time to the wild, untamed Arizona Territory where survival depends on grit, faith, and the courage to start over. Follow three pioneer families—the Andersons, Colters, and Larsons—as they risk everything for the promise of a new life in a land that demands both strength and hope.

A Dream Unfolding
A Heart Renewed
A Life Restored
A Hope Revealed
Hidden Prospects

Desert Manna Series:
Sometimes the most beautiful love stories bloom in the desert. Set in the growing frontier town of Prescott during the early 1870s, these tender romances follow women rebuilding their lives after heartbreak and the unexpected men who help them discover that second chances at love are worth the risk. Set in Prescott, Arizona between 1871 - 1873.

Beauty for Ashes
Joy for Mourning
Oaks of Justice

Colter Sons Series:
Power, legacy, and forbidden love collide in this sweeping family saga set in the Arizona Territory. The Colter ranch empire has weathered decades of frontier life, but now family secrets and buried betrayals threaten to destroy everything. As five brothers—and one resilient sister—navigate the treacherous waters of love, loss, and redemption, they must decide what's worth fighting for. Set in Prescott and

other locations within the Arizona Territory in 1887 - 1906.

The Reluctant Cattleman
The Roaming Adventurer
The Railroad Magnate
The Resourceful Stockman
The Restless Wrangler
The Resilient Bride

Larson Sisters Series
Meet the next generation! These delightful novellas follow the three daughters of Adam and Julia Larson from the *Prescott Pioneers Series* as they navigate love, courtship, and finding their own happily ever afters in territorial Arizona in 1886 – 1894.

In Love at Christmas
In Love with the Rancher
In Love with the Horse Trainer

Desert Life Media

Desert Life Media: *There Is Life in The Desert*

Entertainment-first Christian fiction set in the Southwest, featuring redemption, family, and faith

Publishing clean, wholesome, and uplifting fiction since 2010

---

desertlifemedia.com

New from Desert Life Media

———

Get ready for heart-pounding western adventure! Desert Life Media is thrilled to introduce R.J. Sloane's debut novel, *The Rustler Hunter*, the explosive first installment in the Harper's Justice Series.

"I've always been captivated by the Harper family from Karen Baney's Colter Sons Series," says R.J. Sloane. "Their strength, loyalty, and unwavering faith in the face of danger inspired me to explore their story further. I wanted to dive deeper into the gritty world of frontier justice while honoring the values that make these characters so compelling."

The Rustler Hunter delivers explosive action, unshakeable faith, and a touch of sweet romance amid the dust and danger of the Wild West. This thrilling adventure appeals to both action-loving readers seeking high-stakes western drama and romance enthusiasts who enjoy love stories set against the rugged frontier landscape. Experience wild west adventures fueled by faith as the Harper family faces their greatest challenges yet.

Fans of Karen Baney's beloved characters will recognize familiar faces, while new readers will discover an exciting entry point into a world where justice, family bonds, and faith collide in unforgettable ways.

The Rustler Hunter is available now wherever books are sold.

The Rustler Hunter
by R.J. Sloane

When forty-one successful manhunts make you a legend, there's only one way left to go — down.

J.J. Westin, the infamous Rustler Hunter, goes undercover at Arizona Territory's largest cattle ranch to expose the rustlers bleeding it dry. The thieves aren't just stealing cattle. They're trusted cowboys operating from inside the bunkhouse.

What he doesn't expect is Hayley Harper, the tough-as-nails cook with secrets of her own. She's a Pinkerton agent working the same case and the daughter of notorious outlaw Galen Harper.

When their covers are blown, they uncover something far deadlier than rustling. A corruption network spanning three territories. With enemies closing in and bullets flying, the legendary manhunter and the outlaw's daughter must survive the badlands of 1898 Arizona, where trust is deadly and justice comes at gunpoint.

In the shadow of Canyon Diablo, where the historic Aztec Land & Cattle Company's Hashknife outfit controlled over a million acres of the Arizona Territory's most lawless land.

—

Pulse-pounding adventure of Louis L'Amour
with the heart and faith of Janette Oke.

—

 R.J. SLOANE writes gritty western adventures where justice rides hard across the untamed Southwest. Inspired by shows like Longmire and Yellowstone, plus a childhood spent watching classic westerns with dad, R.J. brings authentic frontier spirit to every page. When not crafting tales of territorial lawmen, you'll find R.J. researching the legendary lawmen of the Southwest and the founding of pivotal frontier towns.

Sign up to become part of R.J.'s Posse (newsletter) at:

https://rjsloanewesterns.com

www.ingramcontent.com/pod-product-compliance
Lightning Source LLC
Chambersburg PA
CBHW070807120626
46557CB00002B/739